The Body Double

a long poem by

Jared Harel

Brooklyn Arts Press · New York

The Body Double
© 2012 Jared Harel

ISBN-13: 978-1-936767-14-4

Cover art by Aaron Sing Fox. Book design by Joe Pan.

All Rights Reserved. No part of this publication may be reproduced by any means existing or to be developed in the future without written consent by the publisher.

Published in The United States of America by:
Brooklyn Arts Press
154 N 9th St #1
Brooklyn, NY 11249
www.BrooklynArtsPress.com
info@brooklynartspress.com

Distributed to the trade by Small Press Distribution / SPD
www.spdbooks.org

Library of Congress Cataloging-in-Publication Data

Harel, Jared.
  The body double / a long poem by Jared Harel. -- 1st ed.
    p. cm.
  ISBN 978-1-936767-14-4 (pbk. : alk. paper)
  I. Title.

PS3608.A7288B63 2012
813'.6--dc23

2012023769

2nd Edition

Many thanks to the editors of the journals in which portions of *The Body Double* have appeared, sometimes in different versions:

Apalachee Review, Cold Mountain Review, Ecotone, The Fiddlehead, Harpur Palate, Hayden's Ferry Review, PRISM International, Quarterly West, Slice Magazine, Tin House

You made this man. Now create another.
Create his double and let the two contend.

—*The Epic of Gilgamesh*

1.

Born in Long Beach, the offspring of immigrants,
my first memory is moving away.

My second memory still doesn't fly.
In it I fall and fall asleep.

Before long, my mind is a truck stop. My heart,
whosever knee is near. I cross

the country in search of my father. No luck
for the next twenty years.

2.

Born in Long Beach to a teacher and mechanic,
my mother swears everything

brings out my eyes. My father was swallowed
by the hood of a Buick in 1984, before the Cold War

stalled. I'll keep them
out of this. Consider it a kindness. Love,

don't distract me. I will tell you anything
if you promise to listen.

§

I forgot who
you were, your name
and face,

your place
in my mind
was suddenly

amiss. *Forgive me,*
I whispered.
This is my pad.

*You must be
my sibling. Here
is a mango.*

I reached for you
and felt
only wind.

The sky, I uttered,
is terribly blue.
That poodle

*you are petting
was implausibly
born.*

You said
nothing. The narrative
forbid it.

I showed you
my penis. I pointed
out trees.

§

Confess everything: how you passed out in the prom parking lot,
tuxedo stained and stinking of beer. Renounce all ties
to mind and body. Break your finger to show them

you are whole. Fuck decorum. Swear and stutter. Sign anything
if what you sign with is sharp. Ration your slop. Compliment the chef.
Befriend futility, for it will not desert you. Befriend maggots

and the ghost in your ear. If grilled further, give up your platoon.
Your pets and children. Come clean about that time at the food court
when you got caught staring at Sara Parker's breasts. Admit

how it feels being slapped into love. Then years later,
after rescue or release, when penning your memoir or running
for office, say you were scared but that God spared you.

Tell not a soul what it takes to be free.

§

An existential crisis is bliss

    compared to this: my double

in my twin. Not even
    a queen. We sleep elbows

out, as though our torsos
    might meld, our thighs collide.

We kick and scratch, fight
    over blanket. *That was my*

rib cage. I miss being
    five. He calls me Monster.

I wish him poor health.
    When we dream, we dream

this will go on forever.

    §

We knew he had died
by the state of his lawn,
a half-acre rising
away from itself.

It looked sad
and a little off-putting,
a marine's buzz-
cut grown out

in a home. My double
and I decided to go
there and mow it.
No one wants death

just over the fence.
So we crossed
lawns and began
to trim bushes, uproot

weeds, hack back
blades as they arced
for sun. Then our neighbor
stepped out in bathrobe

and sandals, this faint
twitch of terror
in his face. I eyed
the grass

as though I'd misplaced
a razor. My double
smiled like he'd just
found a tooth.

§

There are tricks to everything,
    none of which I know.

Clever clues like quarters
    glued to pavement: how to rotate
crops, close deals, please

teach me to fix toilets,
    work camcorders, blow smoke
rings, kill with two fingers.

Three years at my father's garage
    and I can't cut a rotor,
change oil. I forget which direction

sets screws free. Lawnmowers
    mow and I know
not why. Light bulbs brighten

while mine remains dim–
    dimming–dimmer, until what's left
I wonder, but to place

    one foot in front of the other.
Do the math, says my double.
    Sound it out.

    §

I slip him headphones
on a warm April day,

say, *This is what I love.*

On the Hudson

a tanker pulls into view.
Suped-up Hondas

thunder down Ditmars,
trunks pulsing

every off-beat. I study
my double's body

for echoes of my own:
a hint of awe

in the dip of his eyelid,
the singular feed-

back of fingers to knee.
How can it be

that we are from
another?

'Twas in another lifetime,
the singer lies.

§

Keep still, I beg my body double.
*How can I paint you with you
bouncing around?*

He flashes a smile,

frowns my frown,
wanders off
to set fire to the kitchen.

*

I begin with background:
a swing-set, a palace.
I paint the first
cloud that pops
in my head.

Through it all
I feel I am dying,
I feel like dying
is what I've become.

*

When I step back,
it isn't half bad—
the sun is sunny,
chain-links link up. I've managed

to make things
nearly as they are
but for that void of a center,
that mountain of snow.

*

Yes? I answer,
and suddenly my double

is nowhere to be found.

He has shattered the mirror
and eaten my leftovers,
left this note
on the counter by the sink:

Forgive me. I despise you.
It looks just unlike us.

§

There is no room for surrealism
in my family portrait. There is no room
for backtalk, for blacking out.
Everything I am happened to me

yesterday. *Yesterday*, my double says,
is the greatest most terrible day of my life.
My double is homeless.

He lives in my home. My double
has no place in my family portrait.
He hates my portrait. He hates

my parents. He ate all the hummus
I bought for the party. He insists we meet
at an undisclosed location
and blink twice when the coast is clear.

§

And it's clear at last, my double
is a looker. Stopped on the subway
by a chick in stilettos. Cornered

at the drugstore to undress
his eyes. *Gorgeous!* gasps a girl
fishing for her pen, while women

working checkout eagerly agree.
Later, my double's co-worker, Marco,
grabs him by the shoulders, pulls

him to the light. *Motherfucker*,
says Marco. *You look normal to me.*

§

The day my body double discovers secondhand clothing,
he sweeps through the aisles of Salvation Army,
and it takes time but he finds his gems: *All Children Can Learn*,
black with red writing. *Justin's Bar Mitzvah*,
paraded with stars. *I lost 40 pounds in just 8 weeks!*
and indeed it is a pretty tight fit. He wears shirts that swear
he's been to Alaska, Montana, Denmark, Haiti,
Barbados, Slovakia. Shirts worn by Bob,

Lucas, Gumby, Raymond, all probably dead
or fired from their jobs as mechanics, exterminators,
landscapers, park rangers, fitness trainers, train conductors.
His Special Olympics shirt: *A Day in Paradise.*
His Geo-Club shirt: *A "rock-solid" foundation.*
He finds button-downs with neon colors,
Bee Gee collars. Jumpsuits and jerseys for teams
never played on, clinics never signed for, schools and summer
camps unattended. Graduation shirts signed lovingly
by strangers. Shirts bearing numbers no longer
in service, shirts bearing services no longer in business.
He is Otis the Plumber, an NRA member,
#49 for the Glenwood Seagulls. A plump older woman
waddles up to him exclaiming, *Forty pounds in eight weeks!*
How on earth did you do it?

§

We spend the morning unloading nose trimmers,
corkboards, cap-racks, duvets.
We slice through boxes, ripping them open
like the bellies of livestock,

laying them flat, entrails removed.
When a new shipment comes
we wheel it down to the Bed & Bath basement
where a radio cranks K-Rock,

"Highway to Hell," and florescent duct tape
traces the floor. Our supervisor,
Leo, soft-tags toasters.
Once a banker on Wall Street, he now spends

his lunch breaks at K·B Toys, searching for a model
of the Porsche he used to own.
Beside him Keith pounds espresso kits
with a plastic price-gun

and hates my guts. Across the table,
unpacking packs of a Black & Decker cutlery set,
we hate him back. Nothing personal,
just the way things go

when you don't go far.
Shift-clock twisted. Punch-card punched.

§

Herman the Juggler doubles as a vendor.
The trapezist trades her tights
for an oversized t-shirt, her wings
for a stack of coloring books.

My body double notices
bottled-water-guy is also the contortionist
and that kid who punched
our tickets to get in. The Human

Cannonball selling toy whistles
is the Reptile King peddling popcorn,
a drowsy python curled
to its barrel. Children shriek,

small, manic hands hammering for more.
In this makeshift tent
over centerfield, he does not believe
they can be the same: sword-swallower

and security. Tightrope walker
and girl with the lisp. Even the ringmaster,
after the finale, removes his top hat
to break down the set.

§

Since true emotions are inarticulate
and a tear is sincere only
by definition, I shut down
to find out the story, get the facts

by factoring out. My girlfriend
hates this: one-word answers,
the incessant silence, my double
all snowy like a broken TV.

She wonders what he's thinking,

what I think of her outfit.
She turns to the mirror when he fails
to respond. Then one night

after screwing, she screams
I'm leaving! and straightens herself,
searching for her bra. By the time
she's down the block, I see

she means it. He sees she means it
but can't see what she means.

§

My body double tells me
I'm away on business
and won't be back
for quite some time.

Meanwhile, he's agreed
to read my mail,
pick up the newspaper,
just to be safe.

He insists it's no trouble
walking my dog,

dating my girlfriend,
raking the leaves

around my refinished deck.
If I need to call,
I should try
my own number,

unless it is Sunday,
in which case,
my mother's.

§

Double shall be and not be Me, my dress, demeanor, and all other characteristics naturally instructed upon or implied by Me. Double shall not be himself, nor anyone else, nor disfigure nor deface the Me he is being. Double shall act as, and when necessary, react in a manner approximating, Me. Double shall pay for all clothing, surgery, weight training, hairstyling, and any additional cosmetic requirements necessary for accurate doubling. That Double is a lesser version of Me does not give Double the liberty of appearing as such. However, if Double's fashion-taste is deemed intolerable, Double shall pay Me the reasonable costs of garments being provided for by Me. Double shall smoke and thereby inhale three (3) packs of Camel filtered cigarettes per day. In addition to the aforementioned services, during the term of this employment, Double is to ensure that the entire premises, including the range, refrigerator, other appliances, bathroom, closet, cupboards, mattress, floor coverings, and especially the kitchen table is kept clean. If Me is destroyed, damaged by fire, gunfire, smoke, water, or otherwise disabled, dismembered, or abused, or if Me needs to vacate the premises for an extended period of time, Double is hereby instructed to be Me even more overtly, a Me beyond Me, a Me-er Me. Double shall not sublease or abandon his position without the prior written consent of Me. However, in the likely event that Double is destroyed, damaged by fire, gunfire, smoke, water, or otherwise disabled, dismembered, or abused, Double is obligated to hire or obtain a double Double that will observe and comply with the *Standard Procedure for My Body Double* attached hereto.

§

We punch the wrong buttons, put faith
in a manual for an obsolete model, products reduced
to a few passive grunts. Tech-support tells us
to right-click this, reinstall that. They speak

apprehensively as though we've taken hostages
and will blow them sky-high if our printer doesn't print.
Still my body double insists our issues
are metaphysical. He carves meats with a remote-

control cleaver, stumbles in with a fifth
of vodka, yelling "Spacebar! Lord told me spacebar!"
One day it may register how little we believe,
how our lives happen beyond our defiance.

I'll be out fishing with our phone.
When it rings, I will think: *We have finally caught one!*

§

Picture a spider the size of a toaster.
A high slider. A wild pitch.
A kiss is a kiss is a kiss is a fist
so consider what's missed

with wincing, what goes unsaid
with tongue in cheek.
There is nothing to say
for those who startle, who flinch

at the sight of a soiled syringe.
Check their pulse after chasing them
with a chainsaw. Their hearts
as you utter it isn't

benign. To hell with skydiving,
tickle a gorilla. Learn to forget
life's lessons. Embrace the jolt
you knew was coming.

§

1.

My body double goes
to The Home Depot
to buy materials
to build an ark.

He likes the shape
of its hollow smile,
the smell of sawdust
like a vital resource

up in smoke.
An ark? asks the boy
in the bright
orange smock,

then cuts past hardware
over to lumber.

2.

My body double goes
to The Home Depot
and blacks out
in lumber.

He wakes to a panic
of trained professionals,
a woman pricking
his delicate wrist

asking for a name,
a date of birth,
if he recalls drinking
or taking pills?

I remember, he answers,
I'd like to buy lumber.

§

My body double
moves there,
lives off the sand:

*All desert is
is what it isn't,*
he thinks,

and for the first
two weeks he burns
like a rose

in a barren arboretum,
sinks so deep
even the stars

forget themselves.
But with the coming
of thunder

he buries him-
self, sleep

in his eyes, dreaming

between. The sun
is a shawl. Each
grain his grain.

He sees an oasis
and turns
away.

    §

My body double dies
in a single-engine plane crash

and suddenly I have
some explaining to do:

how exactly my double
took off for Chicago,

vanished from radar
later that day. Later that day,

I call my mom to say
sorry I died out in Wyoming,

would you mind not taking

questions from the press?

I almost phone my father, a pilot
in his own right,

to ask if an open-casket
is out of the question,

whether poor visibility
was a plausible cause?

Before long, hordes of reporters
climb my fire escape,

desperate to hear
what not being feels like,

and if heaven was worth
all those flames.

§

Double and people will come
to depend on you: untimely soul-
mate swiped on the turnpike, dazed
neighbor in the center

of your couch. You may find yourself
suddenly helplessly helpful.
You might dole out sedatives

or fresh-baked scones. It is terrible

to think what gallops inside us,
what splits and quarters our soldiers
whole. No longer a loner, that lip-
twist is textbook affection,

a stock symptom of giving
a shit. Soon you'll reform strippers,
food-bank for the poor. You may even
mistake me for God's hungry son.

§

Three DUIs and seven
misdemeanors later,
I spot him at the wedding
of a mutual friend.

It is clear he's on something,
twirling his wrists,
trying to grind
with the Maid of Honor.

And while I know
I should probably
pull him aside, offer water
before he nips

another drink,
or the mic, or the ass
of an unsuspecting
grandmother,

I stand there laughing
like it's all far away.
After all, he may be
destined for greatness.

NOTES

The epigraph from *The Epic of Gilgamesh* arrives from the David Ferry translation, *Gilgamesh: A New Rendering in English Verse*. New York: Farrar, Straus and Giroux, 1992.

'Twas in another lifetime are song lyrics from Bob Dylan's "Shelter from the Storm." Copyright ©1974; 2002 Ram's Horn Music.

ABOUT THE AUTHOR

Jared Harel lives in Astoria, NY. His poems have appeared or are forthcoming in such journals as *Tin House*, *Ecotone*, *The Threepenny Review* and the *American Poetry Review*. He holds degrees from Binghamton University and Cornell University, and plays drums for the NYC-based rock band, *The Dust Engineers*.

Printed by Libri Plureos GmbH in Hamburg, Germany